NAMING LOVE

Geraldine Mitchell

Naming Love

ARLEN
HOUSE

Naming Love

is published in 2024 by
ARLEN HOUSE
42 Grange Abbey Road
Baldoyle
Dublin 13
Ireland
Phone: 00 353 86 8360236
arlenhouse@gmail.com
www.arlenhouse.ie

978–1–85132–319–7, *paperback*

Distributed internationally by
SYRACUSE UNIVERSITY PRESS
621 Skytop Road, Suite 110
Syracuse
NY 13244–5290
USA
Phone: 315–443–5534
supress@syr.edu
syracuseuniversitypress.syr.edu

Typesetting by Arlen House

cover image
by Lisa Molina
is reproduced courtesy of the artist

Contents

7 *Acknowledgements*

14 Oh
15 Home Movie
16 On the Wane
17 Need to Know
19 Forecast
20 Soured by a Poisonous Rant on X …
21 Grave Music
23 Granuaile
25 That Thing with Feathers
26 Resolve
27 Sightings
29 Sky Writing Summer's End
30 Random Notes in Favour of Snow
32 Darling Buds
33 Love in a Damp Climate
34 Bare Bones
35 Of Fire and Water
38 Bedroom Ghazal
39 Reconnect
40 Bóithrín
41 Folly
42 Dummy Run
43 Out of Nowhere
44 Leaving the Festival
45 Fall from Grace
47 Saying It with Flowers
48 Promises
49 Under the Lime Tree
50 Moon
51 Heart to Heart

53 Double Glazed
54 Off Balance
55 November First
57 In Spate
58 Cull
59 Quest
61 Uncharted Waters
62 Missing
63 Listening to Reeds
64 At the End of the Day
65 Day Trip to Inishturk
66 The Return
68 Spindleshanks
69 Sextet for a Composer Pictured as a Tree
75 Final Audit
76 Night Crossing
77 Without

80 *About the Author*

Acknowledgements

Grateful acknowledgement goes to the editors of the following journals and anthologies in which these poems, often in earlier versions, first appeared: *The Cormorant, Crannóg, Cyphers, Hive, The Irish Times, The North, Poetry Ireland Review, Poetry Salzburg Review, Southword, The Stinging Fly, The Stony Thursday Book, The Storms Journal.*

'Bóithrín' was chosen for the Kiltimagh Poetry Trail in 2023.

'Saying It with Flowers' was shortlisted for the 2022 Poetry Meets Politics Competition.

'Need to Know' was placed second in the 2021 Troubadour International Poetry Competition.

'Uncharted Waters' was one of five winning poems in the Dedalus Press poetry postcard competition (2021).

A version of 'Darling Buds' was included in *Local Wonders: Poems of our Immediate Surrounds,* edited by Pat Boran (Dedalus Press, 2021).

'Bedroom Ghazal' appeared in *Days of Clear Light: A Festschrift in Honour of Jessie Lendennie,* edited by Alan Hayes and Nessa O'Mahony (Salmon Poetry, 2021).

'Home Movie' was commissioned for the 2021 Shorelines Arts Festival, Portumna, in response to a photograph by Orla Kennedy.

'Listening to Reeds' was part of Fingal Libraries' Celtic Trees Project, 2021.

'Grave Music' was included in *Metamorphic: 21st Poets Respond to Ovid,* edited by Nessa O'Mahony and Paul Munden (Recent Work Press, 2017).

A huge thanks to Sean Borodale, Paddy Bushe, Jane Clarke, Ted Deppe, Maura Dooley and Kerry Hardie who all generously found the time to read my manuscript in its final stages. My gratitude always to poet, artist and friend Aoife Casby with whom the vital poetry conversation continues. And to my daughter, Lisa Molina, for the cover image.

This one is for
Samuel

Naming Love

a blackbird knaps
the flint of my heart,
sparks fly

the past is too much when the present is thinning and the future grows shorter by the day, and the weight of the past pulls you back, holds you up, a child stopping the seesaw, a chubby-cheeked, mollycoddled Billy Bunter of a boy, leaving you helpless, suspended over the void like when the cable car stalls and you're left up there swaying, sickeningly high above a pine-blackened valley with a huddle of strangers you haven't so much as a language to share with, let alone anything to say, and it wasn't your idea to come on this trip anyway. Oh, the past is a sack stuffed with worn-out emotions that shouldn't weigh anything, no more than a handful of feathers, comforting, soft, a pleasure to sift through, but you're back on the ground with a jolt and your feet sink into the snow with the weight of the bag on your back and you look around for somewhere to dump it, but the scrapyards are closed for the season and the landfill's charging an arm and a leg and you need those intact for the last few miles left to go. Oh the past is so heavy at two and at three and at four and at five until light starts to filter through the crack in the curtains and it's time to make tea, lean into another day.

Home Movie

What I liked most were the colours
of the film I played in my head
that long year of sadness and darkness
and death. What I liked was the yellow.

What I liked was the knowing
it would be there when I woke
because I'd made it
out of another time.

I liked the trees. An old oak,
defiant, incandescent with prayer,
overgrown saplings, strappy and eager,
their whisperings, the wait.

I liked adding birdsong, a breeze, then
slowly turning up the light, the way
the sun came up every day without fail.
What I liked most was knowing it was there.

On the Wane

Such agitation, such trouble
and strife on this earth of ours while
out my window over the hill to the east
a sickle moon reclines, her hands behind her head,
chews the fat with Venus slung from her big toe,
casts about in lazy circles for a place to hitch her web.

Need to Know

where did you go in the night was it
dark was it cold where you were out
there on the sea in the night was there
wind did it rain what did you see in
the night on the sea in the rain did you
meet your mother did you see yourself
coming back going under where did you
spend the cold hours before light where did
you go all those years was it cold were you
afraid of the dark the salt water going under
never up could you see were you lonely did
you talk to the stars were there stars or
a moon did you eat were you thirsty
what did you see were you afraid

seabirds
face into the wind

waves explode
like outraged snow

FORECAST

It lasted for three days and nights, the storm
that ended as we slept, our sleep sunk deep

in the deepening silence, stunned senses
lulled by an absence of racket, stacks of noise

keeled over, lifeless now as fallen trees;
salt clotting the windows, lace patterns

obscuring our view of the sea.
The youngest child was first to wake,

lay spellbound in her cot, was first to hear
the robin's all-clear note, its strident signal

that the world had not quite ended yet.

Soured by a Poisonous Rant on X I Sit in Silence Under Lofty Trees

after James Wright

I turn off iPad, phone, unplug
the internet, open the back door.
The wounded beetle is trying to get in.
It's been here many times before – I recognise
the dent on its inch-long, pitch-black back. Its
twig-dry legs scritch-scratch the cardboard I've been
keeping handy to transport it to the hedge. I walk on,

find a place to sit under the poplars' whisperous canopy,
try to unravel the sonic tangle, the busy conversations
in the trees and in my head. Nothing makes sense.
Then an oriole lets out its mating call, each note
a golden key, a starting place from which
to offer up my silence in atonement,
hope it will be heard.

Grave Music

According to the *Tibetan Book*
of the Dead, although a body
will not come alive again once
the heart has ceased to beat,
for seven weeks the corpse still hears,
each day more faintly, until our
voices can no longer reach it.

But what if that body, although
dead to us, and mourned, slipped
from one realm of sound
into another? What if a
different music filtered in,
earthier, its volume slowly
rising as the coffin lowered

inch by inch into the ground?
What if Orpheus' music were playing
still, trapped in the strata
of the underworld, between silt and sand,
mingled in the soil we walk on?
Or plays itself through roots,
worm tunnels, tendrils

fingering the dark, faint
murmurings, soft susurrus
trickling through the dank
conglomerate of clay?
And what if our own music,
made and played by human hands
and hearts, were nothing but

a quest, a search for harmonies
from another space and time?
The fiddler at the graveside,
the jazz quartet, the marching band –
all echoes, subtly caught, of airs
we sometimes think we hear
on starry nights.

GRANUAILE

I try to imagine you out there, unruly
sister, truculent survivor, old seadog

rhythmed by moon and tide. Your safety
the raging seas, their briny routes

and choppy paths, the ocean roads
that mapped your mind. The creak-crack

of masts your soundtrack; the billow
and pitch of the rigging your dance;

the sweet taste of salt on your tongue,
a tangle of wind round your heart.

wood smoke
weaves
the indigo night

to a blanket
of dark longing
mingled voices

thread
a rug of trust
a roof of song

That Thing with Feathers

Hope used to stick like a bone in my throat,
it was a rope round my ankles, a hole in a boat.
It snagged on the briars of my tangled mind,
I could feel its heart batter. I wanted to believe,
to shout out its name, but it morphed into
candy floss, marshmallow-soft, a basket
of puppies, a card in the florist's shop.

No longer on the verge of extinction,
hope's back from the brink, down
from its perch, been sharpening its beak,
talons are long now, and fierce,
its feathers resplendent as fire. Listen
as it breaks through the bars of the cage
that we made. Hear its sky-rending cry.

Resolve

O the mind, mind has mountains
– Gerard Manley Hopkins

Put a foot on the mountain
follow the mist that rags high slopes
worry grey remnants of cloud
swallow the wet breath of sheep
side-step the claggy drop
tumble arse over elbow to the water's edge
climb through your head
scale the steep bluffs
craggy imaginings

look down

see the moon's alter ego
a parched meadow hallowed with gold
an estuary festooned with spangling squalls
the restless rush of lush grasses
wind in the manes of runaway horses
thundering through the valley
as sheep lift their quiet heads to watch

Sightings

When you walked
into my dream
without knocking

left the door
open behind you
no greeting no

how have you been
I was dreaming of you
how you'd gust into a room

let the door swing
in your wake
turn heads

like just now
when you barged in
and said

did you see
the kingfisher
the way it slits the river

open
pulls a blue thread
lets through the flame

but when I turned
to say yes
you were gone

even solitude’s ache
is softened by sun
a busy glitter on the sea
warm skin and sparrows
pragmatic on the breakfast table

Sky Writing Summer's End

This fractious child is tired of learning letters,
has grabbed the lot, flung them high,
hurled them wide to make up words
in a language only she can read.

The scattered alphabet drifts a blue-
domed sky, fistfuls of black confetti,
a languorous glide and soar above
the cushioned warmth that holds it up.

The small girl feels a gentle shower
of jumbled meanings on her upturned face,
fluttered from the swirl, from the wheeling
dance of indecision. *Will we? Won't we?*

Who's in charge? Shall we go now?
Is it time? Balletic questions written
plain as ABC by a turbulence of circling
cranes on the immense September sky.

Random Notes in Favour of Snow

because *one must have a mind of winter*
white as, pure as, soft as, quiet as

night magic, morning curtains leaking gleam
the child in us expectant, silenced

cars tucked up, muffled under puffy drifts
bird tracks etching dance moves

snowflakes vanishing on eager tongues
snowmen, snowballs, carrots, hats

the taste of gloves, the smell of wool
compacted crystals screaking under boots

thinning dreams of arctic blue
then snowmelt
calving icebergs pure as, white as

the garden
is beginning to itch

under the weight
of winter's blanket

the grass is a dance
of shaggy mountain goats

the tickle of roots
too much to contain

Darling Buds

Out of dry twigs
the jut and peer
of green,

time-lapsed
extrusion
from patient trees,

sharpened blades
pushing
through still-dank earth,

a cast of white
snagged on the blackthorn's
surreptitious spikes,

spiders' nightgowns
thrown out
to dry.

Love in a Damp Climate

A heart does not snap in two
like a biscuit
straight from the packet

before moist air
weakens it
teaches it

the mercy
of silent
crumbling

Bare Bones

Without memory there is no story to tell.
Without story there is no memory.
– Kapka Kassabova

It's only the snatch of a story
and it isn't mine – a bride jilted
on the day of her wedding,
the groom and his lover riding away
to a priest in the next parish
who married them
before they fled on to Dublin,
England, America ...

Or so the story goes,
the one I was told, a story
preserved without radio or newspaper
or any record other than
words spoken and repeated,
the story passed on
not as caution or scandal
– though that too I'm sure –
still holding the pain
and the hurt,
the driving necessity
of love, its cruelty.

Yet who knows, who can ever tell
the true story
what really happened
under the shadow of a mountain
in the teeth of gales
in the hardship of subsistence.
Only the heartache remains.
Only the love.

Of Fire and Water

i.m. Eavan Boland

i

I wait and watch the cracked red
plastic watering can fill up,
the yellow hose administering
its morning panacea, a transfusion
the garden has been holding out for.

A jostle sloshes to the top, threatens
to spill over. How are we supposed
to hold it in, now that we have lost
the shame of welling up in public places,
of naming love, and naming it again,

clapping it out in nightly rhythms
among strangers, or silently, alone,
weeping under bursting trees
as birds scribble song after song
on the sky's rinsed roof?

ii

When I lit the candle on the windowsill
that bleak morning awash with light
it was as if the sun would not let its rival shine.

But there it stayed all day: a delicate fiery finger,
a spire of flame – resolute, intense – a lone voice
reaching up, ungraspable, unquenchable,

until at last the flare began to gutter,
pulled back into the dark weave
of the wick, leaving only an acrid plume
to interrogate the empty space.

01 May 2020

birds all silent
nothing

to crow about
gulls circle

like snowflakes

Bedroom Ghazal

Rain needles the window like hail across the bedroom,
    drives sharpened points hobnail across the bedroom.

A single thrush stakes out the dawn with song,
    ribboned air that sails across the bedroom.

Of all rooms in the house this holds most mystery,
    No Entry in bold letters nailed across the bedroom.

Secrets slip between plump pillows, sealed or shared,
    or open with intent, tell-tale across the bedroom.

Burning with remorse a woman watches
    her lover's puckered face, pale across the bedroom.

O bring back peace to this most sacred place where love
    like orchids must be tended, frail across the bedroom.

Reconnect

'I talk as slowly as I walk,' our guide said slowly as we coiled our way to the top of the village, to the sparrow-pecked flanks of a Romanesque chapel, the rough remains of ruined castle walls, fractured creatures lying open to the skies and to the prying eyes of drones that filled the air like gnats. We waited for a lull, for our bodies to replenish, our lungs refill with thinning air, for pink stain to seep back through our ashen cheeks, pinched nostrils open wide again. 'Now place your palms heart-height against the sun-warmed stone,' she ordered, her birdlike frame leant forward on her stick. 'Close your eyes, hear the chip-chip-chip of chisels, feel skin tear, ripped strips of cotton bind around your bleeding hands, blistered from the mallet's seasoned grip.'

Bóithrín

We walk
under a dizzy roof,
the new moon resting
on a nest of feathers,
torn cloud black around
its crescent bulb.

We walk
bareheaded
in the tumbling
firmament, balanced
on a grain of dust.

We walk
an unlit country lane,
fill each other edge to edge.

Folly

I have fallen in love
with a tree.
At my age.
Imagine.

Dummy Run

I'm practising, rehearsing
a landscape without me
while I can.

The view from my window
is pure geometry –
the curve of the hill,

the crest and swerve
of bent trees, low angled walls,
the roof's gable.

Phone wires loop, stretch,
swoop to the shore, to the sea's
relentless homecoming.

The birds are all avid
for this year's nests,
busy and vociferous

they hover in the corners
of window frames
where I am not.

Out of Nowhere

His back was warped from bending,
tending other people's broken pipes, their
blocked drains, from digging pits for carrots
and potatoes to see him through the winter months;
his dream was of floating in the Aegean Sea, diving
loose-limbed and sun-burnished through warm water.

His face was lined beyond his advancing years, but
when he glimpsed his profile in the big house windows
what he saw was Adonis, or Odysseus
the way he was portrayed in the old school textbook,
or Rock Hudson in *One Way Street*.

His heart was long sealed beyond attachment,
a shrunken spud. But in his memory, some days,
he caught sight of the boy he held hands with
one day on their way to school.

Leaving the Festival
for Anto

As I packed the car to drive north, alone,
in the absences of that Sunday morning,
in the emptiness of an ending, of all endings,

in the inevitable scattering, your text pinged in:
still with us but fading away very peacefully,
stark news I was in no way prepared for.

With what force then the foam of hawthorn
smothered fields and hills in its white blooming,
how loud it shouted look!

feast your eyes, fill your worn-out senses, purge
your empty oil-stained vessels, rinse your skulls,
be drunk on whin, on the sour smell of dog daisy,

the deep butter shine of flags. Bury your faces
in the airy lace of roadside cow parsley,
lift up your eyes to the hills.

21 May 2023

Fall from Grace

The birds are busy with spring
imperatives – housing and husbandry –

syrinxes on overtime as fox and badger
start their slippered rounds. Past midnight,

a nightingale. At daybreak the golden oriole
makes his royal return, tunes up his flute,

begins the first performance of the year.
All day I sleep and wake, wake and sleep,

cocooned in sonic tapestry, laid out
between cockcrow and kestrel, day-

dreaming the hoopoe's three-hoot loop,
submerged in a confusion of warblers

from the reed-beds close by. So easy
to picture a world we've been erased from,

thin-skinned creatures that we are,
and hoarse from shouting.

a smell in the air
like rust
a restless sky
filling and unfilling
with cloud

Saying It with Flowers

I find a gift of roses
shrouded in cellophane
on my husband's winter grave,
petals tight as children's eyes
when they don't want to be seen,
stems hobbled by underpaid fingers
flexing rubber bands in a draughty shed.

I take them home.
Loosen the ties.
See to their feet.

Still they won't unfurl, display instead
the mute indifference of creatures
with no memory of what it is to smile,
young plants drilled since first leaf
to stand up duteous and straight.

I wrap up snug against the low December sky,
set out in search of winter die-hards,
a handful of daisies to keep the roses company
while the forty-three species of wildflower
I have counted on the ditches
and in the fields around my house
sleep on.

Promises

How the apricots on the tree
outside my window
hold on tight

in the strengthening gusts
as pliant branches
whip them

into frenzied
jiving. And
still they cling,

their stern green velvet
smooth
as river stones.

They have no choice,
must bide their time
until it comes,

the rich, warm, orange,
juice-gorged time
when one by one

they'll plummet
to grass or
gravel,

a melt of sun
and sweetness,
a promise fulfilled.

UNDER THE LIME TREE

Birds converse
on themes which are right
over our heads; at our feet,

red-backed beetles too busy
to listen to the hum of a thousand bees
while our lives sit heavy,

earthbound and enigmatic
as clay purged night after night
by worms. Only a rock would be

heavier, more cumbersome
than flesh in this whistling
soughing, simmering

summer garden

Moon

How is it that this cold, this lost and lonely
mirror ball, this fickle silver coin minted
in the sun's fierce heat, this senseless object
of age-old adoration, can come robbing sleep
when she's already full and should need for

nothing more? A shaft of silent light has startled me
awake, her hands are round my neck, her silky fingers
slipping from the cut glass bauble that traps
the evening sun and sets it splintering. Moon's
rainbow shards are faint as rain. I step

into the pewtered garden under a rash of stars,
hear night sounds of sleeping trees, lay
a finger on my pulse, begin to measure
loss in years, love in generations.

Heart to Heart

It's 3am – I'm shuffling childhood
memories like a pack of cards. I cut the deck,
deal myself a random hand, another for my
former self, the child I must have been.
And so begins our drawn-out
predawn game of snap. We try to match
our cards, dig side by side with spades,
sometimes in the garden, more often
on the beach. Quibble over what a club is:
weapon or fun place to be with friends. Agree
that diamonds are forever – but not for us.
When the joker cracks open the dark
it's well after six. With a spiteful kick
and a flip of the sheets he starts tossing
our cards to the floor. Hand in hand,
heart to heart, we turn on him, run him
from the room, fall back to sleep as one.

corn flattened
trees cowed
a heron skulking
in the corner
of a flooded field

Double Glazed

against the cutting wind, the
ruthless rain outside, I press

a steaming mug against my cheek,
sit to watch the bushes dance

their manic dance. Six sheep
huddle in the lee of an old

stone wall – through misted lenses
I make out their muffled contours

dull with mud. News of war
bursts from the radio, sluices

over, round and into me. The sheep
will wait, as they have learned to wait,

for this north-westerly to pass,
for all this to be over. Sounds of

bomb-blasts rock my sheltered study,
sirens whine.

Off Balance

after reading Kerry Hardie's Where Now Begins

The tilt of the earth,
its winter shrug,
the recoil back to sleep.

The way weather is
with no clothes on,
naked fact or slow

disrobing –
cloud on/cloud off
sun in/sun out.

We hang
in the nothingness,
in the everyness of our universe,

the vertigo
of all that is beyond, all
we will never know.

November First,

and there's a pitter-patter
in the silver poplar's buckled
branches as a passing gust

of divilment twists dry leaves
from their hinges, edges them
in fitful free-fall

to the ground. The sound
is unfamiliar, unexpected, new.
Gentle, not quite liquid,

not solid either – I close my eyes
and it's flittered tinfoil,
a curtain made of plastic

bottle tops, a bamboo dream-catcher,
or a snow globe softly shaken
in my mind and suddenly

it's winter – I open my eyes again
and all the leaves are gone, the bare boughs
skeletal, ghostly in the faltering light.

trees are open
cages where birds
in safety
sing their limits

In Spate

There are no river gods, whatever you've been told.
No goddess either. The muddled waters lost their faith

before faith was, missed their footing, plunged down
gravity's sheer ladder from bee-sipped hills to heartless

ocean, swelled from one-ply thread to flailing hawser,
from feeble dribbles moon-bright on some far-off slope

to this, a murderous herd locked in feral madness,
a neck-long, back-long rage of self-annihilation.

This river will not see you light a candle on the bridge,
the flowers you throw will waltz a moment, disappear.

Rivers know no gods. Appease them now.

Cull

As light breaks, first notes splinter.
In the long night's stagnant air
I had begun to gather up the years
– voices and faces, places and songs.

I can feel them now, all silky
as they slither hand over fist
into the dark pouch of spent desires,
the deep cave of secrets.

Quest

The birds were late this morning,
the day broke grey and the wind
was black. I swept myself up,
tried to remember what shape I was
but my heart was sore as back and back
I groped for the pieces, tried to remember
the first time I found my mother gone.

I know three sleeps: the first is blue
and deep, the second full of sand.
The third is smaller, shallow, a crab
in one corner, claws up, watching me,
waiting to see what I will do.
Sharp as knives fear's bony fingers
close around my heart. The crab froths
as it gasps for air. It holds my stare.

When all is sung and danced,
when all is lost and found again,
when everything's tied up with twine
and the black wind's done,
when the last rooster's crowed
from the top of the highest tree,
that's where I'll lay me down to rest,
sad mother. I'll find you there.

O bonsai heart
loosen your love knot
let the snipped twigs
grow

Uncharted Waters

Under cover of night
and rain's soft blanket,
a snail sets sail from the heights
of the town hall's tufted guttering,
down tranquil slate-grey waters
towards the street below.

Poor snail, a world's weight
heavy on her shoulders, domed load
lop-sided on her sluggish form
as she makes the slow night crossing,
uncertain traces silvered
by an intermittent moon.

Missing

A boarded-up house, a leaking ship,
a blindfold woman, an empty shell;

windows broken, slates fallen,
birds nesting in the chimney stacks.

A door left open in a storm,
rain blowing leaves through the kitchen

to the hall; turning down a corridor
finding all the doors are locked;

turning down a corridor
finding that it isn't there.

LISTENING TO REEDS

The wind is from the northwest again
and I have found my favourite place
to shelter, under the shaggy overhang
of a stand of *Arundo Donax,* a giant reed
whose restless growth has served us well:
flutes carved and panpipes cobbled
from its hollow stems; slender whittled slivers
conjuring the rounded sounds of clarinet
and saxophone, the bagpipe's plangent call.

I clear my head, close my eyes,
let the reeds' own music play –
a crackle of just-lit twigs, a drumroll
of skittles, the clatter of dry rain, magical rattle
of jostling tubes. I have strayed into a world
not mine, trespassed on an alien frequency
where the coat-hanger clack of bones
every so often softens
to the whisper of sifted sand.

At the End of the Day

The journalist is talking to camera
but I am transfixed
by the progress of traffic

at her back,
red, white and orange,
a constellated smirr,

evening rush hour
in November
when it hasn't stopped raining for weeks.

Some cars sit
waiting
for permission

to turn
over the bridge
to the safety of home

while others are left
poised on the edge of night,
a hand in the small of their backs.

Day Trip to Inishturk

We head to the back of the island
as though to the back of a book
in search of index and endnotes;
past plots of banked-up earth; past
the last house, a lone shirt
flapping its frayed grey arms.

Fulmars stack the cliff face
in niched order, or sail
aimless as lost letters
over the scalloped cove.
The sea is in turmoil,
puffins whirr and dart.

Back from the edge, sprawled
between stone, sand and grass,
a fledgling plover, flushed
from its nest by rain.
A skua in the space above.
Peregrines on patrol.

As if we did not already know
about survival;
as if this was not
the purpose of our journey.

The Return

In the dream they are always walking towards
        or into: the sea, the road, the lane, the haggard,
gate and yard, old house. There are open arms,

harbour walls held open to embrace, a five-bar gate
        between stone pillars slowly opening. Dogs appear,
they bark, glance at one another, unsure yet

swirling in excitement, barking, barking, barking,
        the way dogs bark arrival in every exile's dream.
And they are always walking towards or into:

sea, road, lane, haggard, gate and yard, the narrow
        kitchen door, a fresh loaf cooling, always,
faces turned and open, always laughter.

dip your pen
in the sea
today

write the story
of a happy
childhood

summer curtains
in a glimmering arc
distant dog-bark

sleep

Spindleshanks

how perfectly positioned
a sheep's legs are: distaffs
in fine balance, ready
for the long night's spinning

Sextet for a Composer Pictured as a Tree

for Michael Gallen

1

As he talks about
those quiet moments,
the early shift when
his wife goes back to sleep
after the predawn feed,

he describes how he sits
in the kitchen's kindly warmth,
his sleeping child strapped to him;
how in his waking head
an orchestra finds space to play.

And when he tells of that near holy place
opening in his mind, his arms
take flight in a Vitruvian arc, describe
a leafy canopy generous enough
to house the full orchestra.

2

Moulded to the sturdy curve,
the stout tree's rounded trunk,
a bat pup's snug and sleeping.

Umbrellaed above, the tree's full crown,
its splendid *ceann* with room enough
to fit the players lurking in the overstory.

Soon they'll rustle their way into
the shifting air, the light that's yet to come.
For now it's in the textured dark

each one sits, each instrument a whisper
to itself, silent sounds within the holding limits
– leaves, twigs, branches –
of the music maker's threshing mind.

3

A trunk, a tree, a quiet sky, a bird's beginning,
a tuning, a listening, a call, an answer,
a quarrel of crows

and again
silence

layered and milling, particles
preparing to capture and carry
whatever is sent their way

4

And the snug child
sleeping
still

5

Birds sleep, so still they are invisible,
all browns and greys in the not-yet-light,

then a wingstretch, a feathershake, an eye-
blink until one by one they are

revealed, spread throughout this atrium
of branches, each in their assigned place.

Somewhere too a roosting owl, stern lookout,
focussed ears and swivelling head alert

to notes not yet issued from the tree's
emerging tapestry, the leaves' collective quaver.

6

Starry dome embroidered with flowers
the feather soft brush of hand or wing
the warmth of cheeks under lips' soft touch

flowers unfurl under water
seaweed billows on an inching tide

the indigo kitchen
fills with light,
the child stirs.

Final Audit

take me by the shoulders
    pin me to the line
hold me up to heaven
    tell me if I shine

beat me with the carpet stick
    shake me till I'm dry
hold me till the shaking stops
    tell me not to cry

Night Crossing

Stepping stone to stone
across the night again, I reach
the fiercest stretch of rapids

when a rush of wind rings through
my bones and they are glass
and you have found the stops to make me

sing, though who you are I do not know
– not human, bird or animal – music maker,
that's for sure, magician of the raindrops' forest

drumbeat, commander of the beads of moisture
poised mid-spill after a sudden squall, orchestrator
of my tears' impending fall, each one on impact

bursting multi-coloured into shards, each shard
flown up and up through shoaling leaves,
birds now and singing, singing when I wake.

WITHOUT

i.m. Michael Viney 1933–2023

without definition
without detail
without the loving gaze
        (where beauty lies)

without curiosity
        (that dogged path)
without taking time, slowing down
        (we'll be a long time dead)

without self-given permission
to dawdle
        (and what's the hurry anyway)

without knowledge

without words
without names for the flowers
in their brimful procession
each spring into summer

primrose, dandelion, forget-me-not,
foxglove, dog daisy, woundwort, self-
heal, meadowsweet, dead nettle, vetch,
loosestrife, black medic, white clover

without caring

without holding a rose to a small child's face
without smelling without touching without
risking your tongue without feasting your eyes
without taking the time without understanding
time as a river without loving the river

without sitting on a rock with your back
to the world while water flows around you
and its music is sweet without birdsong
without knowing where the blackbird nests

without listening

ABOUT THE AUTHOR

Geraldine Mitchell was born in Dublin. After a career combining teaching and journalism that took her to France, Algeria, Spain and, briefly, London, she increasingly divides her time between her home on the Mayo coast near Louisburgh, and southern France where her daughter, son and two grandchildren live.

Geraldine won the Patrick Kavanagh Poetry Award in 2008 and is widely published and anthologised. Her four previous collections, *Mute/Unmute* (2020), *Mountains for Breakfast* (2017), *Of Birds and Bones* (2014) and *World Without Maps* (2011) are published by Arlen House. She has also written two novels for young readers and a biography.